To Patricia Gauch, editor, mentor,
and dearest friend

To Edison, Oskar, and Lily

And, as ever, to my dear Sarah

THIS IS A BORZOI BOOK PUBLISHED BY ALFRED A. KNOPF

Copyright © 2020 by David Small
All rights reserved. Published in the United States by Alfred A. Knopf,
an imprint of Random House Children's Books, a division of Penguin Random House LLC, New York.
Knopf, Borzoi Books, and the colophon are registered trademarks of Penguin Random House LLC.

Visit us on the Web! rhcbooks.com
Educators and librarians, for a variety of teaching tools, visit us at RHTeachersLibrarians.com

Library of Congress Cataloging-in-Publication Data is available upon request.

ISBN 978-0-593-12374-4 (trade) – ISBN 978-0-593-12375-1 (lib. bdg.) – ISBN 978-0-593-12376-8 (ebook)

The text of this book is set in ITC Clearface.
The illustrations were created using pen, ink, and watercolor.
Book design by Martha Rago

MANUFACTURED IN CHINA
September 2020
10 9 8 7 6 5 4 3 2 1

First Edition

Imogene Comes Back!

FROM CALDECOTT MEDAL WINNER
DAVID SMALL

Alfred A. Knopf

New York

Imogene woke up
wondering what the
new day would bring.

To wake up with deer antlers was one thing . . .

and to appear with a peacock's tail was quite another . . .

. . . but now it appeared that the parade of peculiarities would go on.

Though the family was utterly stupefied,
Imogene made the best of things.

With her
long
neck,
she found
Norman's
lost
football.

Later,
she
helped
a neighbor's
frightened
kitten down
from
a tree.

"Hurrah!" cheered Lucy, the maid.

"Wonderful!" said the cook, Mrs. Perkins. "You could work for the fire department!"

Every day brought a new surprise.

When the flowers needed watering,
Mrs. Perkins asked Imogene to help.

"No hose!" she said. "Use
your nose!"

Imogene sprinkled
the lilies . . .

the lavender . . .

. . . the lilacs

. . . and the lady next door.

What was going on?

Was Imogene bewitched? Had she eaten an
enchanted cookie or swallowed a magic potion?

"I don't care *what* it is," Mother bellowed. "No child of mine will be a beast, a bird, or a bug!!!"

"Now, what are we going TO DO ABOUT IT?"

"Donate her to the zoo," suggested Uncle Alphonse.

"Send her to art school!" offered Father.

"Enough is ENOUGH!!!"
Mother howled.

Then—

THUD!

The next day at breakfast,
Father drummed on the
table while his eggs slowly
turned cold.

Uncle Alphonse gnawed
at his fingernails.

Mother dabbed at her forehead and twisted her hankie into knots.

Norman had his camera ready.

What would Imogene be today?

But there she was!! IMOGENE!!
Her nose, her face, her *self*, once more!

Everyone rejoiced.

Especially Mother.

Until . . .

suddenly–